FAMILY MAGIC

FAMILY MAGIC

MICHELE EMMY

ARMLIN HOUSE

ArmLin House Productions
P.O. Box 2522, Littleton, Colorado 80161-2522

ISBN: 978-1-958185-28-5

Cover Design by Wendy Spurlin Designs
wendyspurlin.art

Printed in the United States of America

First Edition

*To moms everywhere.
Hope you can claim a few moments for yourself.
You've earned it.*

Family Magic

Tina made it halfway through the battle before getting shot. Decaf splattered across the classifieds, dripping over the edge of the kitchen table and onto the baby's forehead. Megan let out a howl that would terrify a werewolf, thrashing her two-month-old legs in indignation.

Katy and Josh dove for the foam dart, kicking and clawing as if it was a piece of the true cross and not an ill-considered bribe from the dollar store. Tina grabbed Josh's shoulder just as the phone shrilled.

"Just what do you think—" Tina began over Megan's screams, but Josh wriggled away and vanished down the hall. A moment later, Tina heard the rhythmic boom of Katy's cowboy boots against her younger brother's door.

"Stop that!" Tina yelled as she reached for the phone. "I mean it—" Tina realized she was shouting into the receiver. "I mean, hello."

"Tough morning?" Joanne sounded sympathetic. "If you need to cancel—"

Tina jounced Megan against her shoulder, but the motion only made the baby angrier. In one of those rare and horrifying moments when she saw her life with unremitting clarity, her eyes took in the piles of dirty dishes, stacks of unwashed laundry, and the thick film of dust that coated the furniture like newly fallen snow. The puppy had shredded one of Megan's new booties and was working hard on the second one, and the trail of pink fuzz scattered across the carpet would have led Hansel and Gretel home in a heartbeat.

While Tina hated the thought of anyone seeing how poorly she was managing, it was better than suffering through another interminable afternoon alone.

"Misery loves company," she yelled into the receiver, hoping Joanne could hear her over Megan's screeching.

* * *

"Those cookies are too good to be true." Tina crammed another one of Joanne's chocolate-chip marvels into her mouth and started gathering paper plates.

"I'll do that." In her usual efficient manner, Joanne cleared the dishes and tackled the sticky spots before Tina could object. "Why don't you take a long, hot shower and lie down?" Tina held her breath as Joanne maneuvered the sleeping baby onto her lap, but Megan barely stirred.

Laughter sounded from the backyard. The children had dashed outside with their picnic lunch and were taking turns on the swing set. Turns!

"How do you do it?" Tina burst out "Not the cookies!" Tina wailed. "Josh and Katie never stop fighting unless your kids are here. And this is the longest Megan's slept since she was *born*."

"She's beautiful, Tina." Joanne ran a finger across Megan's damp curls. "If I had your talent, I'd fill the house with pictures of her."

Tears started down Tina's cheeks. "I haven't painted anything in five years, unless you count the bathroom."

Joanne gave her shoulder a gentle squeeze. "Give yourself time. Once they're a little older—"

"That's the trouble." Tina dabbed her eyes with a crumpled napkin. "While they're growing, I'm disappearing."

She sucked in her breath. She had just committed the cardinal sin of young suburban motherhood—admitting unhappiness. Now

Joanne would tell her she suffered from post-partum depression; she was iron-deficient; she should go back to work. While all that might be true, Tina knew her despair came from a far deeper place than the physical ravages of new motherhood.

Joanne said nothing, just picked up the soggy newspaper and started leafing through the Living section. Tina squirmed in her seat. Had she just alienated her favorite friend? Ever since she had met Joanne at a neighborhood playgroup last year, she had not felt quite so lonesome.

A bright yellow flier slipped from the pages and drifted onto the table.

"I thought I noticed one this morning," Joanne said. "You're lucky, Tina. These classes don't come around too often."

Tina reached for the advertisement. It slid through her fingers in an unfamiliar way, as if it was not really newsprint and ink but some exotic substance she had never felt before. It smelled nice, too, like freshly squeezed lemons.

Motherhood taking its toll?
Feeling overwhelmed, exhausted, and unhappy?
Try our Simple Spells for Stressed-Out Moms.
Satisfaction Guaranteed.
Family Magic, Inc.

The phone number was too blurred to read, but Tina recognized the address of a church-turned-community center a few miles away.

She quirked an eyebrow. "Is this one of those Mantra things? Give-me-a-month's-grocery-money-and-squirm-on-a-torturous-metal-folding-chair-until-your-bladder-bursts-and-I-will-teach-you-the-secrets-of-the-universe?"

Joanne laughed. "We sprawled on cushions in a church basement. Plush, comfortable cushions. And talked. And ate, and ate, and ate…"

She pointed to the cookie plate. "If you think mine are good, you've never tasted Glinnie's."

"Did they let you go to the bathroom?" Tina demanded.

"I was nine months pregnant with Susan. I *lived* in the bathroom."

"Don and I tried something like this once." Tina lowered her voice, even though the children were still outside. "Katy was almost due, and he thought it would be a good idea to—you know—iron out the kinks before she was born."

Megan whimpered, and Joanne stuck a chocolate-smeared finger in her mouth. "What happened?"

"We got there late because Don wouldn't ask for directions. The seats were full so we squatted by the door, listening to other couples snipe at each other." Tina grimaced. "Worse than afternoon talk shows."

Joanne's eyebrows rose. "Didn't the leader straighten them out?"

"He encouraged it," Tina said with her mouth full. "'Get it all out in the open,' he kept saying. 'That's why you're here.'

"When the last pair besides us started going at it—he accused her of having affairs and she went on and on about his physical limitations—Don and I just *looked* at each other and snuck out the door."

A wistful feeling flooded through her. It had been a long time since she and Don could simply exchange glances and know what the other was feeling. "We checked into the first motel we found and ironed out the kinks all by ourselves."

Joanne chuckled. "Did you get a refund?"

"No, but for once Don didn't mind. He said he got his money's worth." Tina blushed. "Afterwards, the leader sent us a card and the cutest little yellow sun suit. Katy lived in it all summer, and so did Josh when he was born. It brought back such fond memories for Don and me, every time they wore it. I wanted it for Megan, but," Tina waved a hand at the stacks of household detritus, "I can't even find *myself* anymore."

Tina meant that last statement as a joke, but she could tell Joanne wasn't fooled.

"Glinnie's class changed my life," Joanne said. "Why not give it a try?"

Tina shook her head. "I've never gone in for that kind of stuff. I mean, honestly, Joanne—Black Magic?"

She set down the flier, but it clung to her fingers like a contented cat.

"Not Black Magic," Joanne said. "Family Magic."

* * *

Tina thought she had tossed the flier as soon as Joanne left, but all day long it popped out at her from the oddest places; crammed inside the diaper bag, wedged beneath the baby wipes on the changing table, curled against the half-empty cookie plate. Each time Tina snuck another chocolate-chip cookie, she felt her resistance crumbling.

Satisfaction Guaranteed. Even Don couldn't argue with that. As for Family Magic—it probably didn't mean magic at all, just some New Age, psychobabble parenting philosophy. And getting out of the house one night a week sounded like heaven.

At dinner Tina barely heard as Don went on about his day, which included an altercation with a co-worker and a business deal gone sour.

"You're not listening!" he complained.

"Sorry." She pulled her attention back to the table. Josh and Katy were dropping peas into their milk, giggling as they rose to the surface. Josh ran out of peas and grabbed a handful from Katy's plate. Katy screamed and jabbed him with her fork. Milk frothed across the table and pooled on the floor.

Don gave an exaggerated sigh. "Aren't you going to *do* something?"

Tina ran to the sink. Somehow she was not surprised to find the bright yellow sheet peeking at her from beneath the dishrag.

"I would, but—" she tossed him the sponge, "—I'm late for class."

* * *

Tina eased into a parking space next to a white Volkswagen bus whose bumper sticker read, *My Other Car is a Broom*. A sleek BMW, an assortment of mini-vans, and a station wagon that had seen better days lined up in front of the cozy brick building.

The sun was just beginning to slip beneath the horizon, and the sunset was one of the most startling she had ever seen. She paused to admire the delicate pink clouds, edged with streaks of azure and gold. Six years ago, she would have dropped everything and pulled out her sketchpad. Six years that sometimes seemed like sixty…

Sighing, she picked up Megan's carrier and started up the steps, walking cautiously in her unfamiliar high heels. The smell of lilacs filled the air, though it was far too early for them. Tina gave an appreciative sniff and opened the door.

The large room was warm and pleasantly shabby, with a wide picture window and a faded carpet that felt soft beneath her feet. All the folding chairs had been stacked against the walls. On the floor, just as Joanne had described, sat an assortment of enormous cushions. The only unclaimed pillow, a mulberry cotton with worn gold fringe, was halfway around the group. Tina edged her way through a tangle of diaper bags, strollers, a stationary walker, and a set of pink-and-blue bouncer seats that held a pair of whimpering twins. She put Megan's carrier on the ground and lowered herself onto the cushion. It *was* comfortable. At least Joanne had been right about that.

On her left, a smart brunette whose tailored wool suit screamed, "I'm an executive," chatted briskly on her cell phone, her only concessions to motherhood the enormous dark circles under her eyes that no amount of make-up could conceal.

Tina's other neighbor, a heavyset middle-aged woman, sat stiffly on her cushion with her arms folded. Dressed in faded charcoal sweats, with a helmet of iron-gray hair, she resembled a medieval knight in full armor.

The rest of the circle contained an assortment of mothers as varied as the patches in a crazy quilt. Tina noticed a thin woman with thick glasses already poised to take notes; the young mother of twins, whose cushion overflowed with baby paraphernalia; and an Earth Mother type in a tie-dyed tee shirt and peasant skirt changing her toddler's soggy cloth diaper. Earth Mother's neighbor, an impeccable redhead whose designer handbag had cost more than Tina's monthly mortgage payment, edged her leather pillow as far from the mess as possible.

A final burst of sunlight illuminated the room. Tina's eyes widened as a woman materialized from the brightness. With her long, silver-blonde hair and graceful carriage, she could have been anywhere from thirty to fifty. She struck a nice balance, neither polished nor frumpy, and a welcoming smile lit her pleasant face.

"Hi, I'm Glinnie," she told them. "Looks like everyone's here, so let's sign in." She handed a small blue notebook and a silver pen to the mother with twins. Twin-mom, who was bouncing the pink twin while rocking the blue one's carrier with her foot, looked totally unglued. As her fingers curled around the pen, she seemed to relax.

"What do you want to know?" Twin-mom asked.

"Your name, your children's names and ages, and what you'd like to get out of this seminar," Glinnie replied.

"I'd like to *get out* of this seminar," Tina's gray-haired neighbor hissed. The venom in her tone shocked Tina. Before she could reply, Executive-mom scrawled something illegible and passed her the notebook. Tina drew in her breath. The dark smudges beneath the woman's eyes had all but vanished.

She wrote her name with the silver pen, feeling a sudden urge to fill up the dark blue pages with glittering mountain peaks and shooting stars. Just like the mural she had planned for Katy's room, but had never had time to begin. Well, why not now? Eyes sparkling with anticipation, she offered the book to her grim neighbor.

Ignoring it, the gray-haired woman raised her hand. "Does the class fee include our books?"

Glinnie's lip twitched. "You got time to read?"

A titter ran through the room. Iron-gray flushed.

"I didn't mean to embarrass you," Glinnie apologized, "but most of these moms can't find ten minutes to clip coupons out of the Sunday paper. It's a miracle they talked their husbands into staying home tonight. If I sent them home with books, what are the chances?"

Iron-gray glared at her. "Well, I no longer have a husband, and I haven't seen my kids for days, so I can read all I want."

"I'll make you a list," Glinnie promised. "Anything you can't get at the library, I'll lend you."

Iron-gray started to protest, but Tina dropped the sign-up book on her lap. Her harsh expression softened, and she stopped mid-sentence.

As each woman introduced herself, trying to put into words what she hoped to achieve, Tina noticed a growing similarity. Different as they might appear on the surface, the undercurrent of each monologue was the same; as if somewhere along the convoluted road of career and marriage and motherhood, each of them had left some essential part behind.

"Before we begin, the bathrooms are there," Glinnie pointed down the hall, "the tea is my own special blend, and my daughter made the pumpkin cookies."

"Just what I need, Domestic 101," the Executive mom whispered. "I should have stayed home and looked at briefs."

Tina was pretty sure she did not mean underwear. Execu-mom seemed to think Tina was an ally, possibly because of the high heels. Tina didn't have the heart to tell her that the puppy had snacked on her tennis shoes and this ancient pair of pumps was all she could find.

She hoped it wouldn't turn into the kind of class where they had to express themselves by moving around, and wondered if anyone would notice if she kicked off the uncomfortable shoes and tucked them under her cushion.

"Make yourselves at home." Glinnie spoke as if reading Tina's mind. "Take off your shoes, feed your babies, enjoy the snacks. Just don't talk while I'm talking and we'll get along fine." A loud wail interrupted her. Twin-mom was nursing the blue twin, and the pink one felt she had waited long enough.

Glinnie scooped up the screaming twin and held her out to Iron-gray. "You take the first turn, okay?"

"I didn't come here to hold babies," the older woman protested. "I came to get my teenagers to behave, and my ex to pay child-support!"

Glinnie plopped the baby into Iron-gray's unwilling arms. "Wrong attitude," she scolded. "If we moms don't help each other out, who will?"

Either Iron-gray hadn't lost her mothering knack, or Glinnie had somehow enchanted the fractious twin, for the baby smiled up into Iron-gray's indignant face and babbled something that sounded like a compliment.

The woman's anger melted like a popsicle in the sun. "She's adorable," Iron-gray told Twin-mom, whose anxious expression relaxed.

Glinnie held up a rainbow-colored flier. "We'll meet four times."

The glamorous redhead waved a pale pink paper. "Mine says three."

"The last session is our class potluck," Glinnie explained. "No one's missed it yet."

"What do we eat?" Iron-gray muttered. "Snakes and toads?"

Glinnie's clear laugh rang through the room. "If you want. Me, I prefer lasagna."

She walked around the room, meeting each of their eyes in turn. "Here's the gist. Mothers are the most powerful people on the planet. We bring life into the world, and we raise the next generation. That's a pretty big deal, right? But instead of feeling competent and purposeful, we often feel overwhelmed and insecure. My job is to help you get your confidence back—and maybe, a little bit more."

The thin mom with thick glasses and a clipboard raised her hand. "It takes a village to raise a child. From a global perspective…" Village-mom's voice buzzed like a mosquito as she cited sources.

Tina smothered a yawn. She remembered students like this from her college days, whose sole purpose seemed to be to wrest control of the classroom from the professor and present their own agenda.

Glinnie held up two fingers. Although Village-mom's lips still moved, no sound came out. "You are so right, Roberta," Glinnie said. "Why don't you meet with other village-minded moms after class. Maybe you can organize some meals for *her*." She gestured to Twin-mom, who snored gently from her cushion.

The stunning redhead, who reminded Tina of a fashion model, raised a delicate pink-tipped hand. "If mothers are so powerful," Model-mom drawled, "how come we always get stuck with the kids?"

Glinnie laughed. "Not always. Tonight, my husband has our six-year-old twin boys. His students don't mind—or so he tells me. But then, he has Selective Hearing."

"What's selective hearing?" Model-mom asked, just as Execu-Mom said, "You mean fathers take classes like these?"

"My husband's sessions are even more popular than mine," Glinnie said. "Selective Hearing," she winked and held a finger to her lips, "which we call Shhh, is tonight's topic. Next week we continue with Selective Vision, and we end the classes with Selective Thinking."

Earth Mother nodded sagely. Iron-gray looked disgusted.

"Selective Hearing lets us hear the messages that build our power," Glinnie explained, "and blocks the ones that drain it."

"What kinds of messages?" Village-mom asked, pencil poised.

"Quarreling children, critical husbands," the teacher's gaze shifted to Earth Mother, "nasty in-laws," she glanced at Execu-mom, "unreasonable bosses, unsupportive staff—need I go on?"

"Dead-beat dads," Iron-gray muttered.

"We all have the ability to develop Selective Hearing," Glinnie continued. "So you don't really *need* a potion for it."

"Now she'll offer to sell us a mantra," Execu-mom muttered. "My husband was right. What a rip-off."

"…after years of teaching, I realized how much easier it was for mothers to develop Selective Hearing if they knew how it felt. Otherwise, it's like driving cross-country without a map—doable, but it takes a lot longer." She reached into her dress pocket and pulled out a vial about the size of a film canister. It gleamed like a highly polished mirror. "Selective Hearing eardrops. Two drops per ear, twice a day."

"What do they do?" For the first time, Iron-gray sounded interested.

Glinnie's gaze slid across the group and came to rest on Model-mom, staring with revulsion at her neighbor's unshaven legs and unsupported bosom. Earth Mother's return gaze contained an equal amount of loathing.

"Would you two care to demonstrate?" Glinnie asked.

Model-Mom rolled her eyes but floated to her feet. Earth Mother heaved herself up to join her, spraying whole-wheat zwieback crumbs across the carpet.

"Are they organic?" she asked, as Glinnie unscrewed the top of the bottle and tipped the clear liquid into her ear.

"All natural," Glinnie assured her. She passed the bottle to Model-mom. "And they won't stain."

Model-mom dabbed at her ear with a lace handkerchief. "Why start with hearing?"

Glinnie led the two women to the center of the group. "When you're watching television and a commercial comes on, do you cut the volume or the picture?"

Earth Mother frowned. "We don't believe in television."

"Now, I'd like you to share your impressions of one another." Glinnie winked at Tina. "Get it all out in the open. That's why you're here."

Model-mom's cell phone shrilled, and Earth Mother's frown deepened. "Or cell phones."

"There's a whole box of formula samples in the garage," the redhead hissed into the receiver. "I'm sure the cat hasn't gotten to *those*. I don't care if you're not dressed, find one and feed her!"

"Formula!" Earth Mother spat, as if the word was a deadly poison. "Don't you know an infant needs mother's milk? If I had a dollar for every dirty look I get from women like you when I feed my baby as nature intended, I'd be richer than you. I wish I could take your child home and give her the love and attention she'll never get from you!"

Tina's jaw dropped, but Earth Mother was just warming up.

"I guess flouncing around in a size six suit and driving a Mercedes are more important to you than your daughter's welfare. It's your skewed sense of values that have made this world such a horrible place! And the pity is, when that baby grows up, she'll probably be just like you!"

Tina wondered how Model-mom managed to keep her cool. If someone attacked her parenting and lifestyle with such vehemence, she would be hotter than Brad Pitt.

"Your turn, Paige," Glinnie told Model-mom.

The redhead rolled her eyes at Earth Mother's bushy hair and shabby clothes.

"In case you haven't noticed, we're living in the 21st century. Fathers have always left home to go to work. Well, so can mothers! I like what I do, and I'm damn good at it!

"Your mind is so narrow I'm surprised it doesn't slip out from between your ears. What gives you the right to judge me just because

I live in the real world, and you dropped out two hundred years ago? How dare you deprive your family of all the tools and conveniences of modern life? When your children grow up, they won't believe what an anachronism you are!"

To Tina's astonishment, Earth Mother seemed as oblivious to the insults as her partner.

"How do you feel about one another now?" Glinnie asked them.

Tina steeled herself for the inevitable cat-fight as the two moms rushed towards one another. Her mouth dropped open as they hugged fiercely and started to cry. Model-mom reached into her Prada handbag and pulled out a packet of designer tissues, while Earth Mother tugged an unbleached cotton hankie from her embroidered denim backpack.

"I never dreamed Paige could be so supportive," Earth Mother sobbed, while Model-mom sniffed, "Sierra understands exactly what I'm going through."

The class gawked.

"What did you hear, Paige?" Glinnie asked.

Model-mom gave one last sniff and handed the handkerchief back to Earth Mother. "She understands how overwhelmed I am over this parenting thing, and even offered to help with childcare!" The redhead gave a tremulous smile. "She also told me I looked fabulous and successful, and that Winifred would be proud to follow in my footsteps. I feel like I have a new best friend!"

Glinnie alone did not seem surprised. "And you, Sierra?"

"She admired me for holding true to the traditional values of hearth and home, and said that when Sage and Indigo grew up they would look at me with wonder." Earth Mother's broad smile showed that her aversion to all things modern encompassed dental hygiene.

"Snack break," Glinnie announced, before anyone else could speak. The two moms walked to the refreshment table with their arms around one another, deep in conversation.

Glinnie visited briefly with the other mothers before crossing the room to where Tina stood. "What did you think of tonight's demonstration?"

Tina started to say something tactful, but the words stuck in her throat. Somehow it was impossible to lie to Glinnie.

"It didn't seem honest," Tina blurted. "Neither really heard a thing the other said."

Glinnie looked thoughtful. "In any conversation, people pick and choose what they hear. Despite their antithetical lifestyles, each wanted to feel accepted by the other. Selective Hearing helped them find a way."

Tina didn't entirely agree. "But what if all we ever heard were pleasant things?"

"Selective Hearing helps you hear what you need to make progress in your life," Glinnie explained. "If someone lied to you, or tried to take advantage—"

"Like selling a series of Family Magic classes?" Iron-gray appeared at Glinnie's elbow.

Glinnie didn't seem offended. "You would hear the truth behind their words."

"So when do we put those drops in our husband's ears?" asked Model-mom.

"Or our children's?" Iron-gray crumpled her paper cup and dropped it in the trash.

Glinnie shook her head. "In Family Magic, we work on ourselves."

"But there's nothing wrong with us!" several moms protested at once. "It's our husbands/children/in-laws—"

Glinnie put two silver-tipped fingers in her mouth and made a noise like a smoke alarm on steroids. The babbling ceased.

"Was that witchcraft?" Village-mom breathed.

"Soccer mom." Glinnie looked around the circle. "You've tried changing your husbands, children, in-laws, and bosses. Has it worked?"

The room fell silent. "Then why not try changing yourselves?"

"This is bullshit!" Iron-gray's angry voice rang through the room. "There's nothing the matter with me! I didn't take off with a floozy from the car-rental agency! I don't stay out night after night and make my kids wonder where I am! I need real magic!"

"If you need a different kind of magic, you'll have to take a different class." Glinnie spoke slowly, as if the words were an effort. She pointed out the window to the vacant lot behind the alley. Nearly vacant—towards the back of the scraggly tract, a squat gray building crouched like a baleful toad. Withered cornstalks leaned at crazy angles all around, adding to its spookiness.

The cramped windows were tinted a smoky green and set so high it was impossible to see anything except shadows, grossly distorted shapes which writhed and twisted behind the panes. Tina turned away, her arms dotted with goose bumps.

Iron-gray grabbed her purse and started towards the door. "If I can't put these drops in my ex-husband's ears to make him pay child support, or my teenager's ears to make them pay attention, what good are they?"

"Why don't you give them a try, Irene?" Glinnie's voice was gentle. "You might be surprised at how much power you find within yourself."

Iron-gray shook her head. "I want magic that *does* something, not some namby-pamby feel-good stuff." She brushed past Glinnie, slamming the door. Through the window, they watched her struggle through the weeds towards the grim structure. No light spilled out as she disappeared inside. Tina shivered again. Was it her imagination, or did the deformed shapes dance with new vigor?

Glinnie made an intricate movement with her hands, as if weaving something with her fingers, and flicked the invisible strands after Iron-gray.

"What was that?" asked Village-mom.

"A protective charm." Glinnie sighed. "It's not foolproof, though. If she really wants what they offer, I can't help her."

* * *

Tina tiptoed into the house, trying to be as silent as possible. She needn't have bothered. It was an hour past Katy and Josh's bedtime, but the kids were watching a Dragon Tales video and throwing potato chips at one another. They ran towards her, shouting a list of grievances that would have put Martin Luther's to shame.

After she sorted through the complaints and got them down for the night, Tina staggered into the bedroom and eased Megan into her crib.

Don closed his laptop, yawning. "Aren't you going to thank me for watching the kids?" he asked.

Tina kicked her skirt and blouse to the back of the closet with more force than necessary. "Watch them?" she snapped. "Did you even *see* them?"

* * *

Don left for work in a bad mood, not even pausing to peck her on the cheek as he usually did. Megan was so difficult that Tina lost track of breakfast, and the scorched oatmeal resembled something out of a sorcerer's cauldron.

Katy and Josh took one look at the gray blotches smoking in their bowls and dumped them onto the floor. It was the only thing that united them all morning. To make matters worse, Megan screamed loudly and relentlessly, letting everyone know her agenda was not a happy one.

Tina noticed the shining vial on her dresser as she frantically pulled on yesterday's clothes, and again before lunch when she dashed into the bedroom to change the shirt which Megan had suddenly and violently thrown up on. When she finished rinsing her shirt, she picked up the bottle and opened it. It smelled pleasant, like lilacs.

The volume in the living room increased as Katy and Josh found something new to fight about. Megan's staccato screams punctuated their quarrel like cymbals in a marching band.

What the hell? Tina thought. She filled the glass tube and put two drops in each ear, ashamed of her gullibility. What will it be next? she asked herself. Diamond mines? A bridge in New York?

When Tina emerged from the bedroom the house seemed quieter. She even hummed as she fixed tuna fish sandwiches and Kool-Aid, Katy and Josh's favorite lunch. When was the last time she had heard herself hum? Even the children were listening.

She glanced across the counter. No, they weren't. Katy was pushing a straw into Josh's ear, while he pressed gum into her hair.

Tina started to scold them, then closed her mouth. A smile spread across her face. She opened the pantry and pulled out a can of clam chowder, *her* favorite lunch. One peek in the bassinet showed her that a sleepy Megan was feeling much better. She put the children's plates on the table and sat down with a steaming cup of soup and a magazine, sinking into the quietude as she might slip into a hot bubble bath.

That wasn't a bad idea. Maybe this afternoon while Megan napped, she would treat herself to a blissful soak. Better yet, she could bring Megan in with her, while the others fought or played. Their choice.

* * *

At dinner, Don frowned as he sat on something squishy. "What on earth?"

Tina giggled, and Don wondered if she was laughing at him. "Glitter play-dough," she said. "We made it during Megan's nap."

Don examined his suit for further damage. Tina didn't seem to notice, which annoyed him still further. She had a dreamy expression on her face, as if lost in her own little world, a place in which he had no part. A familiar hurt swept over him, but he stuffed it down and focused on his plate.

He noticed the vial on the dresser when Tina came in after putting Megan to bed.

"What is that stuff?" he asked. Before she could reply, he snapped his fingers. "Let me guess. It's some new-age snake oil from that class, right? How much did it cost?"

Tina didn't bristle as she usually did whenever he asked her a simple question. "It's included in the fee."

"And how much is that?"

"I'm not sure," she replied. "The flier just said, 'Satisfaction Guaranteed.'"

Don's eyebrows rose. "What kind of a way is that to do business?"

Tina shrugged. "Glinnie's way, I guess." She started to brush her teeth.

For some reason, this new calm manner irritated him more than her usual prickliness. "Drugs," he told her. "She'll get you hooked on this stuff, and then when you're dependent…" his voice trailed off when he realized Tina wasn't listening. "Aren't you afraid of becoming an addict?" Tina just smiled and closed the bathroom door.

* * *

Tina was dumping two months' worth of overdue library books into the return bin when she heard a discreet cough. She straightened and saw Iron-gray, the woman who had stalked out of Glinnie's class.

"Hi," the woman said. "I'm Irene, remember?"

Tina's mouth dropped open. Iron—Irene— looked as if she had received a year's worth of makeovers from an exclusive spa. Her silver hair was styled in a new fashion, and her well-cut navy suit looked like something from Execu-mom's closet.

Over the past week Tina had managed to start Katy's mural and conquer the laundry, but her own accomplishments paled beside Iron-gray's stunning transformation.

"You look fantastic! What did you do?" Tina bit her lip, hoping the woman wouldn't take her compliment the wrong way.

Iron-gray seemed too happy to feel offended. "One of my new teachers gave me the clothes," she crowed. "Another cut my hair, and this," she gave her designer bag a loving stroke, "I got with my first alimony check!" She grasped Tina's arm. "Why don't you come with me next week? Learn some *real* magic."

Tina was eager to find out more, but just then Katy and Josh emerged from the stacks, arms laden with picture books.

"I'll think about it." Tina picked up Megan's carrier and started to walk away when a thought struck her. "Those shadows I saw through the windows—what are they?" she asked. "No human could twist into those shapes."

A tremor passed over Irene's face, pale beneath the expertly applied make-up. "I have to go."

"You forgot your books!" Tina called. But Iron-gray had already hurried away.

It was only much later, when Tina sat snuggled on the couch between Katy and Josh reading them a beautifully illustrated Rapunzel, that she wondered what Iron-gray was doing in the Children's Section.

* * *

The classroom buzzed with conversation as Tina climbed the steps for the second time. A pile of casseroles crowded the edge of the refreshment table; Village-mom's attempts at creating community had obviously paid off. Tina added a dish of macaroni and cheese and a plate of butterscotch cookies to the collection and looked around. Model-mom had exchanged her stylish suit for designer jeans and a button-down shirt, and Earth Mother was helping her lower a baby girl into a cloth carrier that hung around her neck and over one shoulder.

"Sierra's a wonder!" the redhead beamed, catching Tina's eye. "With this sling I can do five miles on the treadmill every morning, and Winifred loves it as much as I do. She also takes Winnie to the park with her kids in the afternoons, so I can finally catch up."

Earth Mother smiled, and Tina gasped at the improvement. "I believe in the barter system," she announced. "Isn't it lucky that Paige's husband is a dentist?"

Execu-mom looked envious. "Maxwell's car seat throws out my back every day," she complained. "Would you make one of those for me?"

Other moms crowded around, begging for turns. A flustered but delighted Earth Mother promised to bring an assortment the following week.

Glinnie gestured for them to sit down. "How did your week go?" she asked.

"My mother-in-law came for dinner, like she does every month." Earth Mother said. "But she didn't criticize how I'm raising the kids, or make her usual snide comments about my broccoli and mung bean casserole. She even hugged me when she left and said I was one-of-a-kind!"

Model-mom raised a perfectly manicured hand. "I had to go to a party for one of my husband's colleagues, and not one of their snooty wives lectured me about how they were back to their pre-pregnancy weight in two weeks."

All had similar stories. "The house was so quiet I could hear myself think!" was a common refrain.

Tina's stomach fluttered as she realized it was her turn to share. "At first it was great to see the kids fighting and not hear them," she said. "In fact, the less attention I gave when they whined and quarreled, the less they fought. By the end of the week, we actually started having fun together."

She wanted to stop there, but she could tell Glinnie knew she wasn't finished.

"But all of that peace and quiet gave me time to look at myself," she said in a small voice. "And I didn't like what I saw."

Glinnie gave an encouraging smile. "I know it's not a comfortable place to be, Tina, but it's a great place to be *from*. Usually new students don't find that 'sticky spot' so quickly. You must be unusually talented."

Tina felt a warm glow from the unexpected praise. She had not felt talented at anything for a long time, not since the art classes she had taken in college. Suddenly she longed to hold a paintbrush again, to study a building, a flower, a face, and capture it in color and line...

"Cut your dose of SH drops to one drop in both ears every day this week, and every other day next week," Glinnie told them. "By then, your bottles will be empty, but you'll intuitively know how to listen to what's important and ignore what isn't."

"But they're working so well!" Village-mom voiced the panic that Glinnie's announcement invoked in the others. "Is it prescription? Maybe insurance will pay—"

"It's a tool, Roberta, not a crutch," Glinnie cautioned. "Trust me, you'll be fine." She rose and stretched, causing the shimmery fabric of her dress to send out sparks of light like shooting stars. "Snack time. Let's see what I can conjure up."

The class crowded around the window and watched Glinnie disappear inside the Volkswagen bus. A light flashed, which might have been the reflection of the sunset on one of the side mirrors, and she reappeared wheeling an enormous cooler.

Tina's gaze wandered to the vacant lot across the alley. The clumps of withered cornstalks had multiplied since last week, their twisted lengths nearly shrouding the cinder-block structure. And those monstrous shadows blocking the cloudy windows—had they grown even larger?

Glinnie came up beside her. "What's on your mind?" She opened the cooler, revealing every soft drink Tina had ever seen and several she had not.

"Iron—Irene," Tina corrected herself. "I ran into her in the library. She's doing so well. Sh-she told me I should come with her."

Glinnie twisted the top from a dark-blue bottle. Tina did not recognize the label, a majestic Pegasus flying towards a rainbow. There wasn't another like it, so she chose a diet Coke. "Do you want to?" Glinnie asked.

Tina studied her fingernails. "It's not that I don't like your class, but she has everything she wanted! And I'm still floundering."

"I'd wait until the next time you run into her before deciding," Glinnie suggested. "She might look different once you have Selective Vision."

"What makes you think I'll run into her again?" Tina asked, but Glinnie had already moved on to another student.

* * *

Don pushed his plate away with a satisfied sigh. Tina had been such a good cook before the kids came along, but for the past five years it seemed dinner had been either hot dogs or spaghetti—if she bothered to serve anything besides cereal. Tonight, though, she had produced fettuccine alfredo, one of his old favorites.

"That was the best dinner I've had in years," he said. Somehow the compliment did not come out as intended. His shoulders stiffened as he waited for her to pounce, but Tina only smiled as she started to clear the table. For once, he felt glad she rarely listened to him.

As if on cue, Megan began to wail. Don started to offer to help, then bit his tongue. No matter what he did, Tina never liked how he did it. Years of withering glances and pointed sighs had made it clear that his clumsy efforts could never provide the respite she needed. Eventually, he stopped trying.

Tonight, instead of ignoring him as she scrambled to do everything, Tina gazed at him as if she understood his dilemma. When was the last time she had looked at him that way— as if she really *saw* him, really understood how hard he pushed himself every day to make her proud of him, to take care of them…

"You look beat," she said, with no trace of one-upmanship. Reaching into the fridge, she pulled out a bottle of breast milk and put it in a pan of hot water to warm it. "Why don't you sit down and feed Megan while I wash up? Josh and Katy can clear the dishes and wipe the table."

Don's jaw dropped even further as the kids scrambled to help. When they were finished in the kitchen he read each of them a bedtime story, remembering how much he used to enjoy this evening ritual.

While getting ready for bed, he noticed a second vial on the bathroom counter. It must have come from Tina's class as well. Curious, he reached over and uncorked it. A smell of lilacs filled the air.

Tina had lilacs in her wedding bouquet. He remembered the sun on her face, how she smiled up at him when he bent to kiss her…

He felt a hand on his shoulder and gave a guilty start. "I was just curious. I'm sorry—"

Tina stepped closer and slipped her arms around him. When was the last time she had done that?

"Smells nice, doesn't it?" she said. "Like lilacs."

Don gaped. Usually Tina—'touchy Tina', he had nicknamed her in his mind—jumped all over him at the slightest provocation. Now here he was, going into her private stuff, and she didn't even raise her voice. Come to think of it, he hadn't heard her yell at the kids for days.

"You had lilacs in your wedding bouquet," he said softly.

Her lips curved in a smile. "You remembered." She put her arms around his neck and they enjoyed a long, sensual kiss. When was the last time she had kissed him with such passion?

"Mommy!" Josh's wail could have roused a bear from hibernation. "Katy's writing all over my sheets!"

Don braced himself for Tina to push him aside and rush down the hall. Instead, she chuckled. "Maybe it'll improve her spelling," she murmured, lifting her face to his once more.

* * *

Tuesday morning Tina dropped Katy and Josh at Joanne's house, picked up her friend's shopping list, and headed to the grocery store. Ever since the two friends had hit on this method of marketing, errands had become almost pleasant.

She was studying Joanne's list when she noticed Iron-gray in the produce section. Glinnie had been right. Though the older woman was still well-dressed, this time in a red wool pantsuit, beneath the expensive clothes and perfect make-up she looked haggard and tense.

Joanne had asked for six ears, and the corn looked so good Tina thought she might get some too. She reached for an ear just as Iron-gray came up beside her.

"How's it going?" Tina pulled back part of the husk and frowned. The outside looked good, but the kernels were wormy and rotten. She tossed the ear back onto the pile and chose another.

Iron-gray fidgeted like a toddler who had waited too long to go to the bathroom. She must have leaned too far back against the display, because the tightly packed ears gave an ominous rustle and started to shake.

"I'm learning *real* magic, not the watered-down stuff you're getting. Did you ever get taken for a ride!" She laughed, but the sound held no mirth. "My spells do things—powerful things—" The corn rustled more loudly. Tina edged around Iron-gray to try again.

"Really? Like what?" Tina asked, more out of politeness than real interest.

"Like this!" Iron- waved her hands across the display as if conducting an orchestra. The rustling grew to an angry rumble.

This ear was even worse than the first. She would have to talk with the produce manager.

"They sure don't grow it like they used to, do they?" Tina turned her cart away. "I think I'll check out the squash."

As if taking offense at her words the display exploded, ears of corn raining around them like oversized hailstones. Was it her imagination, or were the ears of corn rising into the air, the corn silks twisting the pieces together to form grotesque shapes, shapes that writhed and twisted in bizarre gyrations...

Tina blinked and rubbed her eyes. They felt odd, as if the Selective Vision drops had formed a protective film across her pupils. When she looked again, dozens of ears of corn lay scattered around her feet. A few rolled towards her, but Tina kicked them aside and started to walk away.

Iron-gray grabbed Tina's arm, but not like she had in the library. This time, it felt more like when Josh watched the nurse wheel in the tray with the shot on it. She gestured towards the ruined display.

"Aren't you frightened?"

Tina shrugged. "It's not my fault if they can't stack vegetables. Besides, with all the money I spend here every week, what are they going to say?" An errant ear nearly tripped her. Tina picked it up and tossed it back in the stands.

Iron-gray's face turned even paler. Hands trembling, she pointed to the sleeping Megan. "A-aren't you afraid for *her?*"

Tina put a box of tomatoes in the cart and smiled at the baby. "If she wakes up, she wakes up. I can always carry her—that baby sling Sierra lent me is a wonder." She checked her list and headed towards the cereal.

Iron-gray hurried after Tina like a teenage groupie following a rock band drummer. She looked around and lowered her voice before she spoke. "Did Glinnie teach you a spell to ward off evil?"

Tina chuckled, until she noticed Iron-Gray's terrified expression. "The way Glinnie explains it, evil things rob us of our true power," Tina said. "We're learning to focus on the important things in life," she touched Megan's cheek, "and ignore the distractions." She gestured to the ruined display.

Iron-gray's face crumpled like a mud pie in the rain. "I misjudged you," she sobbed. "All of you."

Tina looked through her purse but all she could find to offer was a crumpled baby wipe.

"Maybe I should come back," Iron-gray said through her tears.

"I hope so," Tina said insincerely. "We miss you." Standing on tiptoe, she reached for a family-sized box of corn flakes.

"Let me." Iron-gray grabbed half a dozen of the large boxes from the top shelf.

"Thanks, but I only need one."

"The rest are for me," Iron-gray said. "I *am* coming back."

An eerie groan echoed through the store. Megan's eyes flew open.

"Bother," said Tina. "I wish they'd grease those rack things they use to wheel stuff around." She sighed with relief as Megan settled again.

Tina glimpsed Iron-gray at the checkout counter, her cart piled high with corn flakes, corn meal, grits, creamed corn, and a variety of cornbread stuffing mixes. The cart looked like it was sagging, but Iron-gray, head high and eyes clear, seemed oblivious.

* * *

Tina paused on the church steps to admire the sunset, Megan bouncing snugly against her side in the colorful sling. She had taken to wearing the baby as she tackled her household chores, and Megan's screaming fits had almost ceased. Tina wondered if she could persuade Earth Mother to make her one to keep.

She rummaged through the diaper bag and pulled out a small sketchpad and box of pastels she had discovered in the long-neglected linen closet. She didn't want to be late to class, but if she waited for the break the light would be gone.

The Selective Vision tincture had proved every bit as effective as the SH drops, Tina decided as she chose her colors. She had been afraid the magical drops would highlight the flaws in her housekeeping, but they had done just the opposite. Instead of seeing the dust and clutter, she began looking at things the way she used to, when a sketch-pad and not a diaper bag had been her constant companion.

The curve of Megan's cheek, the way Josh's golden-brown hair just brushed the tips of his ears, the hazel flecks in Katy's eyes, so much like Don's…it was as if everything worth looking at leapt to the surface, while the rest faded into the background.

Iron-gray's frantic voice interrupted her thoughts, followed by Glinnie's soothing tones. Tina hesitated, unwilling to stop what promised to be a lovely sketch, but Iron-gray's distress was too pronounced too ignore. She picked up Megan's carrier and went inside.

"…and that was only the deposit. They say they'll waive the rest of the fee if I come back, but if I don't honor my contract…" the rest of Iron-gray's sentence hung in the air.

"Did someone say contract?" Tina hadn't heard Execu-mom come in, her baby tucked against her side in a bright pink sling. Her eyes narrowed as she noticed Iron-gray. "Oh. You're back."

"I wish." Iron-gray's tone was wistful. 'But I can't afford to quit the other class." She scowled at the piece of paper in her hands.

Execu-mom glanced at the document. "It isn't binding."

Hope filled Iron-gray's eyes. "How can that be?"

"You didn't sign it."

The hope vanished. "Yes, I did," Iron-gray mumbled. "In blood."

"Did you sign under duress?" Tina asked. It was the only legal phrase she could remember from the cop shows Don favored.

Iron-gray hung her head. "I wanted to sign. So when she pricked my finger—"

"She pricked it?" Glinnie said sharply. "Not you?"

Iron-gray shook her head. "I was supposed to," she said, "but I guess I didn't move fast enough. I hate needles. So Perdita grabbed it and jabbed my finger, and my blood dripped onto the paper. I saw it," she added, a hysterical tinge to her voice.

"Which finger?" Glinnie demanded.

"This one." Iron-gray held out her hand, the perfectly-shaped nails Tina had admired at the library bitten to the quick.

Glinnie examined them, tactfully ignoring the ruined manicure. "There's no scar."

"Maybe it was the other hand," Irene said. "I can't remember exactly. What's the difference?"

Glinnie continued to scrutinize Irene's hands. "Stephanie is correct," she said at last. "The contract is not valid. You never signed it."

"But I *felt* it," Iron-gray insisted.

"Illusion," Glinnie said. "A real prick, especially one that bled enough for you to sign your name, would have left a Trace."

Iron-gray drew in a shaky breath. "So I can stay?"

"Why do you want to come back?" Glinnie asked.

Iron-gray plucked at her sweat shirt, the same tired garment she had worn to the first session. "Because of her." She pointed to an astonished Tina. "My assignment was to convince her that our magic was more powerful. I tried to impress her at the library, but when that didn't work, they told me to scare her."

Iron-gray took a deep breath. "But she was so brave! All the noises and threats didn't even phase her. When the corn formed scary shapes and attacked her, she never even got flustered. So I figured, if a mouse like her—sorry, Tina—could change so much in just a few weeks, maybe I didn't give you enough credit."

Glinnie patted Iron-gray's arm. "Welcome back."

The unhappy woman burst into tears. "I don't even care about the five hundred dollars," she sobbed. "I'm just so glad to be out of there."

"Five hundred dollars?" Tina was scandalized. "Does it say anything about a refund?"

Execu-mom sniffed the air, grimaced, and pulled her child out of the baby sling. "If she didn't sign, she doesn't owe," she said as she headed for the bathroom.

Tina handed Megan to Earth Mother. "Come on, Iron—Irene," she said. "We're going to get your money back."

"It isn't worth it, Tina," Glinnie said, and there was something in her voice that, had it been anyone else, Tina would have sworn was fear. "Others have paid far more for a glimpse of what they have to offer."

"Maybe not to you," Tina replied. "But the rest of us can't conjure up coolers full of treats. Do you have any idea what it costs to feed teenagers these days?"

She picked up the contract and marched across the weed-choked alley, a reluctant Irene tagging after her. "Why are these cornstalks so withered?" she asked Irene. "Summer's barely started. I wonder if they used a pesticide."

Irene kept her eyes on her worn tennis shoes. "Nothing grows well around them," she said, as they approached the ugly building.

The door swung open before Tina could knock, revealing a short, dumpy woman wearing flowing robes the color of dried blood. Her stringy gray hair was braided into corn-rows, interwoven with small, skull-shaped beads. She reminded Tina of her high school PE teacher, the one who made them run laps even when the temperature climbed over a hundred.

Tina straightened her shoulders. She wasn't fifteen anymore, and she refused to feel intimidated.

The witch's tongue flicked back and forth, reminding Tina of the snake in Josh's classroom. "You brought a companion," she said to Iron-gray, who looked as white as Don when the doctor showed him where to cut Katy's umbilical cord. "That is good." Her pebble-like eyes appraised Tina. "I am Perdita. Why are you here?"

"Because I lost the light." Tina shrugged. "So I figured, 'what the hell?'"

Iron-gray looked bewildered, but Tina's answer seemed to please the witch.

They stepped through the wall of shadows, the door swinging shut behind them with an ominous squeal.

Iron-gray blanched. "We shouldn't have come. You have no idea—"

She yelped as a ghostly face materialized in the gloom. "What is your need?" the chalky face asked, her voice as hollow as her cheeks. "Whatever you crave, we can provide it—for a price."

Tina shuddered. No wonder Iron-gray hadn't wanted to come back. This place was even spookier than the Haunted Maize she and Don had visited while they were dating. She shuddered as she remembered the shrieking ghouls that popped out from behind the hay bales. She'd screamed and clung to Don, and he pulled her close. "Don't be afraid," he'd whispered into her hair. "None of this is real."

Except us, she remembered thinking, as he bent to kiss her. *We're real*.

Tina wrapped the memory around her like a warm blanket, then lifted her eyes to the chalk-faced specter. "You need some WD-40 for those hinges," she said, "and my friend needs her money back."

Chalk-face looked stunned. "Impossible," she hissed.

Tina tightened her grip on Iron-gray's shaking arm. "Nonsense. Every hardware store carries it." She held out her hand. "Her deposit, please, so we can go back to where we belong."

"She belongs here." Chalk-face's tone was adamant.

Tina prodded Irene. "Tell her."

"Th-this place is not f-for me," Iron-gray stammered. "I'm going with Tina."

The witch Perdita put a hand on Iron-gray's arm. Tina noticed that she wiggled her fingers up and down in a repetitive motion.

"Are you certain, Irene?" she purred in her scratchy voice. "You were doing so well." Her fingers did not stop.

Iron-gray hesitated. "Well, I—"

Unconsciously Tina repeated the motion she had seen Glinnie make when Iron-gray left class the first day. Perdita's hands froze as if she had slapped them.

"How did this one get past the Wall of Shadows?" Chalk-face demanded.

Perdita waved her fingers as if a wasp had stung her. "She said she lost the Light. She mentioned our Sacred Place. I thought—"

"Nobody cares what you think!" Chalk-face waved an imperious hand at Tina and the trembling Irene. "There is no going back. We must form the Crooked Chain. Take your places at once."

"I don't think so!" Tina grabbed Iron-gray's arm and looked straight into Chalk-face's red-rimmed eyes. Mouse, indeed! She thrust out

Iron-gray's contract. "You and I both know this wasn't binding. Unless you want to meet in small claims court, you'll give her back her money, and you'll give it to her now."

"Let them go, Perdita," Chalk-face said at last. "The first one showed promise, but she has been warped beyond repair. And this one," she gave Tina a disgusted look, "has been blinded by the Light."

Tina ignored the insult. "If you don't have cash on hand, you can mail her a check," she said. "But if it doesn't come by next week," inspiration struck, "our whole class will be knocking at your door."

"That won't be necessary." Chalk-face pointed to a low table that Tina would have sworn was not there a moment ago. On it rested a gray metal box, whose dimensions paralleled the squat building. "The funds are inside." The lid of the cash box opened by itself. A slender leg poked out, and something large and dark and fuzzy emerged and scuttled across the table.

Irene yelped, but Tina reached out and stroked the tarantula's silky back. "He's a beauty." When the creature didn't object, she held out her hand, continuing to caress its soft fur as it walked up her arm. "You shouldn't keep him in that metal box," she scolded Perdita. "He needs light and air. Besides, if he can get out so easily—" she gave a pointed look at the lean black cat rubbing itself against Chalk-face's flapping robes. "Do you have a cage for him? Or—I don't suppose he's for sale? We looked after the one from the pre-school last summer, and Josh has a birthday—"

"Enough!" Chalk-face hissed like a gas barbeque. Perdita scrabbled through the box and held out a handful of gold coins.

Tina gently nudged the tarantula back onto the table, but it clung to her fingers until Perdita snatched it and flung it back into the cash box. Tina started to protest, but before she could say anything both box and table vanished.

Chalk-face lifted a sleeve, but Tina couldn't see her arm. "Go," she ordered. "And never return."

"You mean it?" Iron-gray grabbed Tina's hand and practically pulled her out of the building, much like Katy's first foray into kindergarten.

To Tina's surprise, the sunset blazed even more brightly as they walked towards the church.

Glinnie had changed her usual format and had them working in pairs. "I'll work with Irene, to help catch her up. Why don't you stay out here and sketch?" She winked. "I'll hold the light for as long as I can."

Was it Tina's imagination, or did the sun flare slightly before settling back to a steady glow? Before she could ask, Glinnie put her arm around Irene's shoulders and led her inside. Tina pulled her sketching things from the diaper bag, so absorbed in her work she was oblivious to the mothers who joined her outside during the break.

"Can I see?"

Model-mom, balancing a plate filled with veggies and dip, stood at her shoulder. Tina wondered where she got the willpower to resist the fudge cake and lemon bars the others were wolfing down.

Tina handed her the finished sketch. She had drawn a rough facsimile of herself sitting on the porch steps with Megan on her lap, the glorious sunset illuminating the fine strands of Megan's hair. At the edge of the piece she added a suggestion of the squat building across the alley, framed in clumps of withered weeds.

"Wow," Model-mom said after a minute. "Are you always this good?"

Tina flushed. "Sometimes I get lucky."

Model-mom set down her plate and fumbled through her handbag. "How much do you want for it?"

Tina's mouth dropped. "You want to *buy* this?"

At Model-mom's nod, her face broke into a smile. "You can have it."

Model-mom raised perfectly plucked eye-brows. "Why?"

"Because you liked it enough to pay," Tina said. "You made my day."

"Tina." Execu-mom appeared at her elbow. "You're a good artist, but a lousy businesswoman. Why do you want it?" she asked Model-mom.

The redhead flushed. "My brother and I own a greeting card company." She said a name that made Tina gasp. "I think it would make a splendid card."

"So you want reprint rights?" Execu-mom demanded.

Model-mom squirmed. "I offered to pay—"

"How much?" Execu-mom asked.

"One hundred dollars," Model-mom said.

Execu-mom laughed. "Are you kidding me?"

Model-mom flushed. "It's not like she's known—"

"Five hundred, for the sketch," Execu-mom ruffled through her diaper bag and pulled out a legal pad. "We'll discuss commissions later."

"It's too late," Tina searched her memory, "Stephanie. I already gave it to Model—I mean, Paige."

Execu-mom didn't miss a beat. "Not reprint rights," she said, making rapid illegible scrawls across the yellow pad. "My client gets ten percent commission on all cards sold."

"That's unheard of!" Model-mom folded her arm across her chest. "We always buy outright."

Tina held up her hand. "The sketch is a gift, reprint rights and all," she said, ignoring Execu-mom's disgusted snort. Model-mom shot Execu-mom a triumphant look and started to walk away, but Tina shook her head. "You can have it next week," she said. "I want to make a copy in watercolors first, as a good-bye present for Glinnie." She hesitated, then asked, "What do you like about it?"

Model-mom ran a finger over the glowing clouds. "The simplicity of line," she began, pointing to the figures. "And the way you catch the peaceful feeling over here, in contrast to *that*," she traced the nearly-vacant lot with a shapely finger, "adds a tension usually missing in this kind of drawing."

Tina drew in her breath. "Do you think you might be interested in more?"

"A series?" Model-mom wrinkled her brow, then instantly smoothed out the creases. "What were you thinking?"

Tina's pulse quickened, but she kept her voice even. "How about a dozen sketches of mothers and children in nature, with varying qualities of light and tone, but each with the sense that the subjects have walked through *here*," Tina ran a finger across the bleak vacant lot, "to find their place in the sun?" She stole a glance at Glinnie, who was chatting with a laughing Twin-mom, and felt suddenly inspired. "We could call them Charmed Lives."

"I like it," Model-mom said at last. "You're on."

Tina turned to Execu-mom. "You're right, I don't know much about being a businesswoman. Will you represent me, please?"

"She didn't give you the name." Execu-mom reached for her pen, but her baby grabbed it from her fingers and ran the tip along her blouse, shrieking with laughter at the expression on his mother's face.

Model-mom held out her hands. "I'll bounce him while you draw it up," she said. "How soon can you have them?" she asked Tina.

"Give her a break." Execu-mom did not pause in her writing. "She's got three kids."

"Do you want them all in pastels?" Tina asked.

Model-mom nodded, and Tina did a rapid calculation. "Six weeks, if none of my kids get colds or chicken pox." She meant that last remark as a joke, but the pen halted mid-scribble.

"I'll put in a chicken-pox clause."

Tina felt suddenly anxious. "How do we do this? Because I can't pay you until Model—Paige pays me."

Execu-mom handed the pad to Model-mom. She must have been able to decipher it because she signed without hesitation.

"Don't worry," Execu-mom said. "I'll take a watercolor too, and we'll call it even."

* * *

Later that night, when the kids were asleep, Tina told Don all about it. "You would have been proud of me," she said, face flushed with excitement.

Don reached over and pulled her close to him. "I'm always proud of you, Tina," he murmured against her hair. His lips brushed the top of her head, then traveled to a favorite spot on her ear.

Megan's cry shattered the moment. Tina started to scramble out of bed, but Don stopped her. Just as he used to do when Katy was newborn, he changed Megan and carried the hungry baby to Tina.

A smile spread across his face as he watched them. "Say, isn't that—" he ran a finger along Megan's bright yellow sun suit.

Tina nodded. "It was at the back of the linen closet, along with my sketching things and driver's license," she said, then bit her lip.

Don carried the sleeping baby back to her crib. "Driving without a license," he teased, as he slipped beneath the covers and took Tina in his arms. "I might just have to ask you to pull over." He nibbled her ear again, and neither spoke for a long time.

* * *

Tina felt a pang as she climbed the church steps for the last time. She placed a batch of cream-cheese filled brownies on the potluck table, heaped with mouth-watering displays of fruit and vegetable salads, twice-baked potatoes, pies, and several variations of Glinnie's favorite, lasagna. Model-mom had relaxed her standards and brought an enormous tray of chocolate-dipped strawberries, and Earth Mother's mushroom and tofu casserole looked almost edible. On the floor beside the table stood Glinnie's enchanted cooler.

Model-mom sighed as she joined the others. "All Winifred wants to do on those eight-month-old knees is lope," she mourned, "and my thirty-year-old feet can't keep up."

Glinnie materialized at Model-mom's shoulder, her plate heaped with a portion from everyone's offerings. "I hired Irene's teenagers to keep an eye on all the toddlers. You just relax and have a good time." She nodded to the porch, where a girl with jet-black hair and a nose ring blew soap bubbles for a delighted audience. A boy with a shaved head and tattered motorcycle jacket was chasing a trio of toddlers around the tiny lawn.

Tina sucked in her breath, but relaxed as she noticed how he took care to stay between the children and the street.

"That's great for tonight, but what about tomorrow?" Model-mom laughed, but her gaze was bleak. "I love my job, but I hate dropping Winifred off at daycare every morning. I know she doesn't get the exercise or the attention that she needs. And Sierra can't help me every day."

"Why don't you hire a nanny?" Iron-gray asked, as she popped a strawberry into her mouth. Tina noticed that her plate, though full of nearly everything else, contained no cornbread.

Execu-mom came up beside them. "Nannies are vanishing faster than the South American rain forests, in case you hadn't noticed," she said bitterly, "and no one is making any effort to save them."

Iron-gray looked puzzled. "You know, when my kids were little," she said, "a bunch of us met at the park every day, or at somebody's house if the weather was bad. If one of us had to go to the dentist, or wanted to get their hair cut or see a matinee, it was no big deal." She sighed. "Those were my favorite years."

The younger moms stared at her as if she had just told them the location of a hidden treasure buried nearby.

"Weren't you looking to earn some money, Irene?" Model-mom's voice was deliberately casual. "Because if you are—"

"I'll pay more!" Execu-mom snapped.

The ensuing babble sounded like someone had put one extra cookie on the preschool lunch table. Even Glinnie, in earnest discussion with Village-mom, came over to see what the fuss was about.

"I don't know," Irene said. "I love kids—especially those too small to talk back—but babies as a career? It's not like I'm licensed or anything—"

"I'll take care of that," Execu-mom assured her. "You can start tomorrow."

"I asked first!" Model-mom showed no signs of giving in.

Irene held up her hands, laughing. "I'll watch both of them," she said. "My two were only one year apart. Besides, they'll have more fun if they have someone else to play with."

"What about me? And me?" Other moms had gathered around, faces hopeful.

"I guess I could manage a few more before school starts, while my kids are around," Iron-gray said. "Come fall, though, you'll have to figure out something else—unless maybe I hire somebody…" The group of moms walked away, talking excitedly, leaving Glinnie and Tina alone.

"I have something for you." Shyly Tina handed Glinnie the sketch. "Not that I could ever thank you enough for what you've given me." She struggled to put her feelings into words. "I thought motherhood was taking me away from myself," she said finally. "I didn't realize it would also bring me back, but with so much more…dimension." She gestured to the sketch. "It's easier for me to draw it than to say it."

Glinnie studied the piece for a long time. "I will treasure this."

Tina knew she meant it.

"Where will you go next?" Tina asked.

"I'm not sure." Glinnie waved a hand towards the street. "When each class is finished, we just pack up the cooler and climb onto the broom—into the bus, I mean—and see where it takes us."

Tina looked out the window. "At least you'll be far away from—" She gasped as she noticed the squat building was missing. Even the cornstalks seemed to be melting away before her eyes. Only a few stragglers remained, surrounded by weeds. "What happened? Where did it go?"

Glinnie joined her at the window. "It's fading," she said. "Just as this place will, after we all leave tonight."

"You mean…" Tina's voice trailed off as she struggled to understand.

"We always travel together," Glinnie said. "I'm not sure if we follow them, or they follow us, but we always end up in the same place. One can't exist without the other."

Tina felt stunned. "But they're *evil*."

Glinnie smiled. "That's your perception. They serve a need, just as we do." She gave Tina's hand a squeeze. "I'm glad you stuck with us, though."

Tina followed Glinnie back to the food table. Village-mom and Twin-mom had decided to continue swapping childcare. Earth Mother, clutching a worn copy of Dress for Success, was starting her own business. "Stephanie says she'll help me with the paperwork, for a share of the profits."

"Gross profits," Execu-mom corrected.

"Whatever." Earth Mother looked across the room at Model-mom, whose yellow voile dress and lace-up sandals could have graced the cover of Vogue. She straightened her back and sucked in her stomach. "Do you think that comes in my size?"

As a parting gift, Earth Mother had brought each of them a sling. Tina handed out copies of her sketch, reveling in the admiration. The pile grew as Model-mom handed out manicure sets, Village-mom passed around *It Takes a Village…* t-shirts, and Execu-mom presented each of her classmates with a personalized leather planner. Iron-gray's gift was the most appreciated—an afternoon of childcare. Glinnie surprised everyone with midnight-blue journals, complete with silver pens.

As the other moms said their good-byes and drifted out the door, Tina lingered, curiously reluctant to leave. "Joanne told me this class changed her life," she blurted. "Now I understand why."

Glinnie hugged her. "I feel the same, every time I teach it." She reached for the last chocolate-chip cookie on the plate, broke it in two, and offered half to Tina.

"Mmm," Tina said, her mouth full. "Joanne was right about these cookies, too. Please could I have the recipe?"

To her astonishment, Glinnie shook her head.

"Sorry, Tina," she said, eyes twinkling with laughter. "But I can't give up *all* my secrets."

About the Author

Michele Emmy lives in Colorado with her husband of 35 years. They have two grown children, but are sadly out of pets at the moment. A former marine biology major, Michele remembers the resident octopus disappearing for days at a time, to be found skulking in a nearby tank. A Clarion graduate and Colorado Gold fantasy award winner, Michele deals with the constant images and phrases popping into her head by grabbing her laptop and tapping them onto the page, where they belong. When not wrestling with imaginary creatures, she can be found messing with her five Instant Pots and thinking--hard--about exercising.

Also By Michel Emmy

Hex-A-Gone
Pieces of Eight

About the Publisher

ArmLin House is a unique publisher and production company. We help you develop your story in a memoir, business book, instructional video, and more. Then we format your story and help you present your work, whether you release it yourself or we do it for you. And once your story is out there, we can help you promote it with written and visual aids.

It's our mission to help our clients succeed in whatever they do. We take your visions and make them possible through coaching and distribution assistance. The products we produce are informational and entertaining. We also help clients market themselves and their businesses. We produce based on your needs, whether it be in print, digital, audio, or video formats. Then we help release it to a worldwide audience.

ArmLin House Productions
contact@armlinhouse.com
www.armlinhouse.com